DATE DUE			
JUL 2 3 2010	JUN 2 0 2017		
AUG 0 4 2010	JUN 2 6 2017		
AUG 1 2 2010	AUG 2 8 2017		
DEC 1 7 2010	JUL 1 6 2018		
JUN 2 8 2011	AUG - 6 2018		
NOV 1 5 2012			
MAR 1 8 2013			
MAY 0 2 2014			
JUN 2 6 2014			
JUL 1 8 2015			
AUG 1 8 2016			
MAR 2 9 2017			

P
F
BRO

Brown, Marc

Spooky Riddles

2010

SPOOKY RIDDLES

Marc Brown

BEGINNER BOOKS
A Division of Random House, Inc.

Library of Congress Cataloging in Publication Data: Brown, Marc Tolon. Spooky riddles. SUMMARY: Witches, skeletons, ghosts, vampires, mummies, and the like are featured in this collection of riddles. 1. Riddles, Juvenile. 2. Supernatural—Anecdotes, facetiae, satire, etc. [1. Riddles. 2. Supernatural—Wit and humor] I. Title. PN6371.5.B76 1983 818'.5402 83-6051 ISBN: 0-394-86093-4 (trade); 0-394-96093-9 (lib. bdg.) Manufactured in the United States of America 1 2 3 4 5 6 7 8 9 0

ABCD   4 5 6 7 8 9

What does a mother ghost say to her child when they get into the car?

Why do skeletons hate winter?

The cold goes right through them.

Why was Dracula put in jail?

He tried to rob a blood bank.

What rides at the amusement park do ghosts like best?

The scary-go-round and
the roller ghoster.

What is the best way
to talk to a ghost?

Long distance.

What does a witch ask for when she checks into a hotel?

Broom service.

Why do witches
fly on brooms?

Vacuum cleaners
are too heavy.

What do bats need after a shower?

A bat mat.

What time is it when a ghost comes to dinner?

Time to go!

What does **a** little witch
hope to get for her birthday?

A haunted dollhouse.

W hat should you do
when you see a ghost?

Hope the ghost does not see you.

How does a witch tell time?

With a witchwatch.

Why don't skeletons go to scary movies?

They don't have the guts.

Why do vampires drink blood?

What do you call a mummy who eats cookies in bed?

A crummy mummy.

Why do witches
wear pointy hats?

To cover their pointy heads.

What yard will kids never play in?

A graveyard.

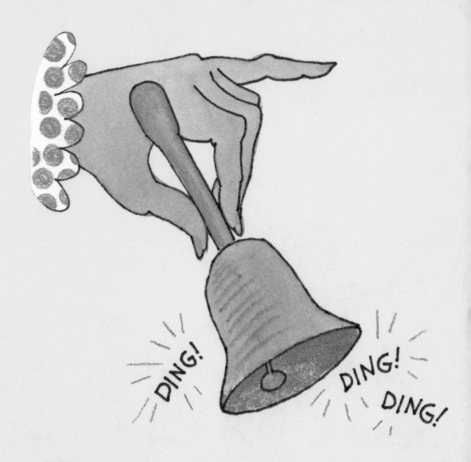

What do you get when you cross
a bell and a bat?

A dingbat.

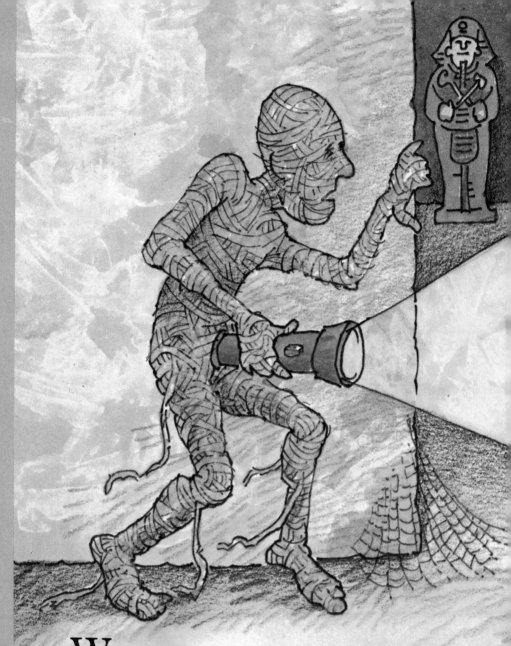

What did the detective mummy say when he solved the case of the missing cat?

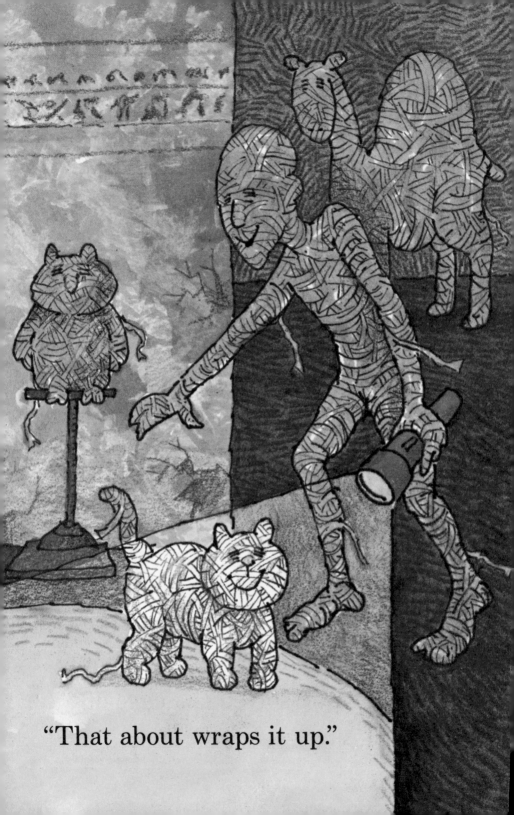

"That about wraps it up."